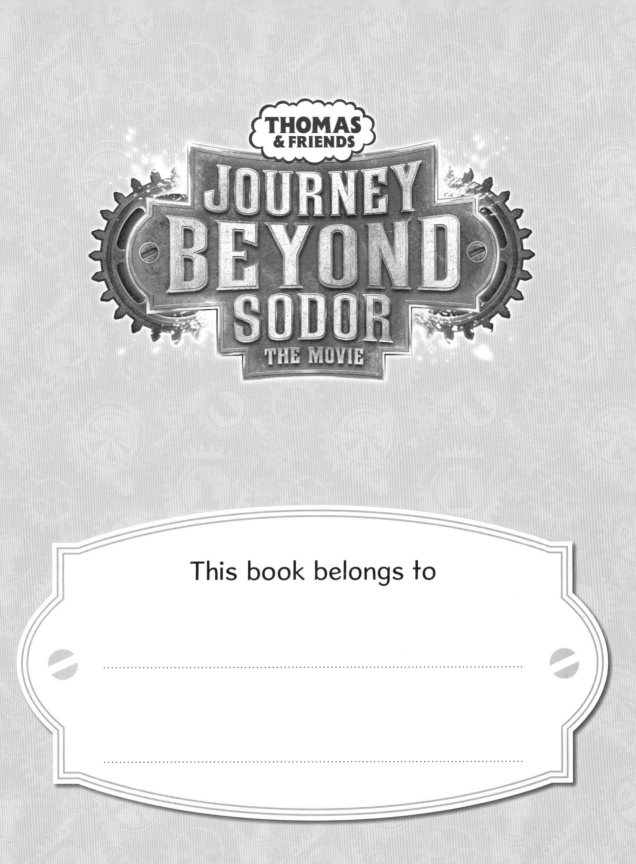

This book belongs to

....

....

EGMONT

EGMONT

We bring stories to life

Based on the original script by Andrew Brenner

Illustrated by Tommy Stubbs

First published in Great Britain 2017 by Egmont UK Limited
The Yellow Building 1 Nicholas Road London W11 4AN

Thomas the Tank Engine & Friends ™

CREATED BY BRITT ALLCROFT
Based on the Railway Series by the Reverend W Awdry
© 2017 Gullane (Thomas) LLC. Thomas the Tank Engine & Friends and
Thomas & Friends are trademarks of Gullane (Thomas) Limited.
Thomas the Tank Engine & Friends and Design is Reg. U.S. Pat. & Tm. Off.
© 2017 HIT Entertainment Limited.

All rights reserved.

HiT entertainment

ISBN 978 1 4052 8768 5
66749/1
Printed in Poland

Stay safe online. Any website addresses listed in this book are correct at the time of going to print.
However, Egmont is not responsible for content hosted by third parties. Please be aware that
online content can be subject to change and websites can contain content that is unsuitable for
children. We advise that all children are supervised when using the internet.

EGMONT

It was a glorious day on the Island of Sodor as Henry rolled into Vicarstown on his way to the Mainland. Suddenly, a signal failed!

Screech!

Henry tried to brake, but he crashed into another goods train.

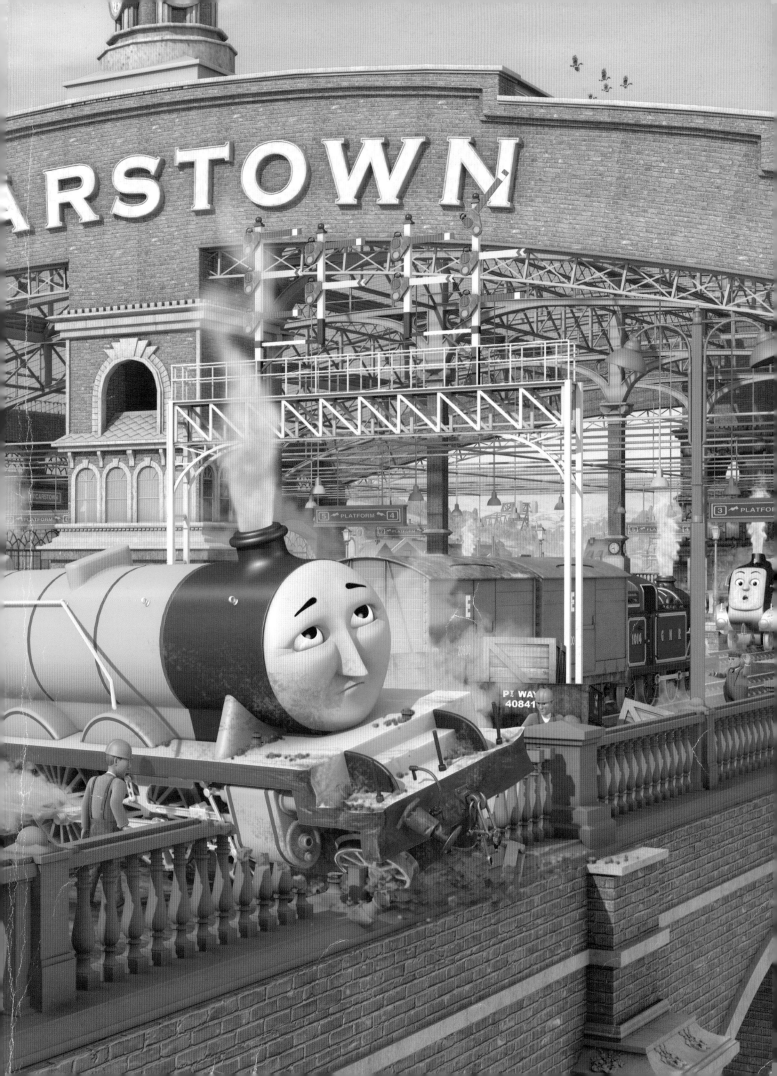

Henry had to go to the Steamworks for repairs. The Fat Controller decided that James would take Henry's cars.

James puffed with pride to be going to the Mainland. "That's a great job. What an adventure!"

Thomas wasn't pleased. James always got the best jobs. And the red engine said he was The Fat Controller's favourite.

Then an idea flew into Thomas' funnel ...

Early the next morning, Thomas went to the Vicarstown Goods Yard, and *he* collected James' trucks.

Soon he was on the bridge to the Mainland. He was excited, but also a little nervous. He didn't know how to find his destination, the Bridlington Goods Yard.

On the Mainland, Thomas met a crane named Beresford.
"Who goes there?" Beresford asked.
"I'm Thomas," the blue engine peeped.
Thomas asked for directions to the Goods Yard, but Beresford couldn't help him. He'd never been there. He could only go up and down a small section of track and spin around. He was a very curious crane indeed. Thomas quickly steamed away.

Later, Thomas rolled into a lonely engine yard filled with old machine parts.

"Hi-de-hi! Pleased to meet you," tooted an engine named Lexi. A shy engine named Theo rolled up alongside her.

Thomas had never seen engines like these. He asked what kind they were.

"We're experimental," Theo peeped.

"It means we're different!" tooted Lexi. "Test models — trial and error."

Lexi and Theo had another friend named Merlin, but Thomas didn't see him anywhere.

"You won't see Merlin," Lexi peeped with a chuckle. "He's a Stealth Engine – designed to be hard to see. Out of sight. Invisible!"

"Merlin can make himself invisible?" Thomas gasped.

Lexi laughed again. "Let's just say he's always 'disappearing'."

With fresh coal in his hopper and a tank full of water, Thomas set off once more. It wasn't long before he rounded a bend and saw an amazing sight — a giant Steelworks.

"I have a feeling we're not on Sodor anymore," said one of the Troublesome Trucks.

As Thomas steamed into the Steelworks, two huge engines rolled up. One was a big tank engine named Hurricane. The other was a diesel shunter named Frankie.

Thomas asked if the engines knew how to get to Bridlington.

"Of course!" said Frankie. "But you mustn't worry about going to the Goods Yard tonight. Uncouple those cars."

"We'll look after them for you!" boomed Hurricane.

Thomas released his trucks and went to tour the Steelworks. Everything glowed and sizzled as molten steel was poured into moulds. Special machines and cars whizzed around Thomas.

"This is the hottest place in town!" Hurricane and Frankie tooted.

When the tour was over, Thomas settled into a comfy shed for a much-needed rest.

The next day, long before dawn, Frankie and Hurricane woke Thomas. They'd already taken his cars to Bridlington.

"If my cars have been delivered, I need to head back to Sodor," Thomas peeped sleepily.

"But we helped you, little tank engine," Frankie tooted. "Surely you don't mind helping us in return?"

Thomas agreed and spent the day shunting ladle trucks and transporting waste from the furnace. It was hot and dangerous work. He couldn't wait to return to Sodor.

But when he had finished, Frankie and Hurricane wouldn't let him go. They said there was more to do – and they locked him in the Steelworks!

Meanwhile, back on Sodor, everyone wondered where Thomas was. James was especially concerned — because he was tired of doing all his friend's work! "I'm going to the Mainland to find Thomas and bring him home," he said.

That night on the Mainland, thunder rumbled and lightning flashed across the sky. Thomas knew he had to escape while Frankie and Hurricane slept.

He rolled through the darkened Steelworks, slowly building speed, and bashed through the gates!

Thomas escaped into the dark woods.

"Are you hiding?" a voice asked. "I love hiding. I'm a Stealth Engine."

Thomas couldn't see anyone but knew this was Merlin's voice.

"Don't worry," Merlin whispered. "You're with the best hider ever."

Thomas felt safe, and the big engines didn't find him. The next morning, Merlin was gone.

As Thomas steamed towards Sodor, he met Beresford the crane again – just as Frankie and Hurricane came around the bend! Beresford quickly hoisted Thomas up and hid him.

Just then, James rolled down the track and met Frankie and Hurricane. The three engines steamed away together.

Thomas knew that he needed to save his friend. He also knew who could help.

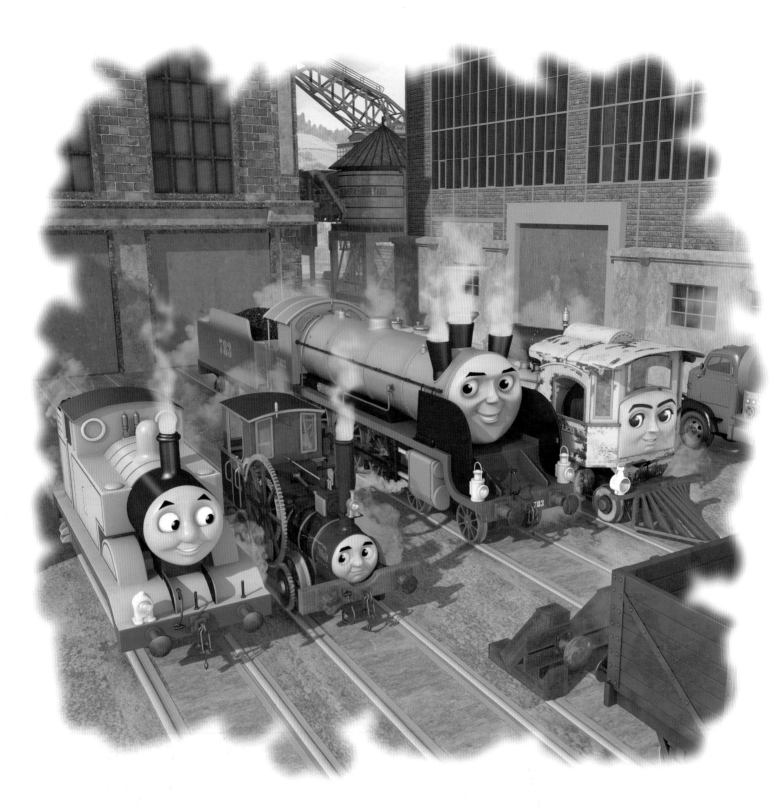

Thomas hurried to find the experimental engines again and
asked Theo, Lexi and Merlin to help save James.
   "But we can't do anything," Theo protested.
   "We can TRY!" replied Merlin.
   "This is the most excitement I've had in ... forever," Lexi tooted.

Theo and Lexi took a flatbed filled with scrap and pretended there was an accident.

While Frankie and Hurricane went to investigate, Thomas and Merlin snuck into the Steelworks.

"James!" Thomas peeped. "We really need to go!"

"Oh, I'm more than ready to go," James puffed. "This work doesn't suit me at all!"

Just then, Frankie and Hurricane returned! They chased James and Thomas into the fiery Steelworks.

Theo tried to help, but he crashed into a control panel. A giant magnet suddenly swung out over the tracks and attached itself to Thomas. It lifted him up and carried him towards a blast furnace!

Theo hit another button to release Thomas. He crashed to the ground and knocked over a vat of molten steel. A fiery puddle spread towards Thomas!

Hurricane sped forward and shoved Thomas out of the way.

The little blue engine was safe, but the big engine's wheels had touched the boiling hot puddle.

"Help!" Hurricane steamed. "My front wheels! I'm melting!"

Merlin quickly pushed Hurricane to safety. But Hurricane's wheels were damaged. He needed serious repairs.

Without Hurricane's help, Frankie didn't know what she would do. "I can't do everything on my own," she steamed. "*Nobody* wants to work here!"

Thomas knew some engines that might.

The experimental engines said they'd be happy to work at the Steelworks. They liked being helpful and useful.

When they were back on Sodor, Thomas apologised for taking James' trucks.

"And I'm sorry I teased you about being The Fat Controller's favourite engine," James peeped. "If anyone's the favourite, Thomas, it's probably you."

"Don't be silly, James," Thomas peeped with a chuckle.

They rolled into Tidmouth Sheds, where their friends were happy to see them again.

"Now there's a sight for sore eyes!" The Fat Controller exclaimed. He was happy to have *all* of his favourite engines back together again!

In the early 1940s, a loving father crafted a small blue wooden engine for his son, Christopher. The stories this father, the **Reverend W Awdry**, made up to accompany the wonderful toy were first published in 1945. Reverend Awdry continued to create new adventures and characters until 1972, when he retired from writing.

Tommy Stubbs has been an illustrator for several decades. Lately, he has been illustrating the newest tales of Thomas and his friends, including *Blue Mountain Mystery*, *King of the Railway*, *Tale of the Brave*, *Sodor's Legend of the Lost Treasure* and *The Great Race*.